STORYTIME
CHRONICLES PUBLISHING

Written by Geoffrey Bolton

STORYTIME WITH DADDY

The Tale of the Old Knight

Illustrated by Adit Galih

"Hey kids!" Dad called from the living room, "I hope you're ready for bed! I'm going to start telling the story without you!"

Three children scrambled into the living room, each wearing their pajamas and laughing as they came. It was story time with Daddy which was their favorite time of day.

"So, who gets to start?" Dad asked, as they piled all over him in the big puffy blue chair.

"Me!" "No, Me!" "You started last time!" "It's MY turn!" came the rapid-fire responses.

"Alight kids." Dad interrupted. "I'll start tonight, and we'll share the storytelling." There was murmured agreement from the children, and then Dad began...

"Once upon a time in a far away land there lived an Old Knight in a Forgotten Castle."

"With a princess!" yelled the littlest one, and at almost the same time the boy shouted, "With a Dragon as a pet!"

"That's right!" said Dad, "And if you remember, Toasty the dragon kept the place warm on cold nights. The beautiful princess Ivy lived there with him. She was always getting into mischief of one kind or another, so the Old Knight was sent by King Gregory of Everlastia to protect the princess while he was away. Princess Ivy loved to explore, but the land was filled with dangerous creatures and people, like the…"

"Evil Witch!" cried the oldest child.

"Evil Gang of Thieves!" exclaimed the boy.

"The Evil Witch was in a Gang of Thieves." Dad corrected.

"The beautiful princess Ivy was being protected by the Old Knight while the Evil Witch and her Gang of Thieves try to capture her. The reason why the Evil Witch was so intent on capturing Princess Ivy was because the Princess had a magic ring she wore on her finger that would grant the wearer special magical powers. The Evil Witch was already a powerful sorceress, but to have this ring would make her even more powerful. Luckily, the Old Knight did not have to protect her alone. Toasty the dragon helped keep them away with his…"

"Rainbow breath!" "Fire Breath!" "Lightning Breath!" the children bellowed simultaneously.

"I'm glad you remembered! Toasty's special breath powers were used to confuse and scare away the Evil Witch and her Gang of Thieves whenever they came prowling around."

"YES!" came the trio reply.

Dad continued, "The Old Knight was hand-picked by King Gregory of Everlastia because he…"

"Had a HUGE sword!" "Wore pink armor!" "Knew Kung-Fu!"

"Yes!" Dad said, "The Old Knight was a highly trained warrior with skills honed for protecting Princess Ivy, with armor and weapons that were magical. He spent many hours each day training to stay fit and studied in the library at night by candlelight. He was an extraordinary Old Knight."

"And he rode a Lion named Leeony!" cried the youngest.

Dad chuckled. "Leeony was the brave mount that carried the Old Knight around. The Old Knight would sometimes go on adventures to try to find the hide-out of the Evil Witch and the Gang of Thieves."

"And look for pretty flowers for the princess?" asked the littlest.

"Magic flowers!" cried the oldest, "That smell super-duper nice."

"That only grow in volcano lava." added the boy.

"Yes! The Old Knight would travel around on his trusty lion, Leeony, looking for the Evil Witch's Gang of Thieves as well as Magic Flowers that only grew in the heart of volcanos in steaming lava beds.

It was dangerous work and he was constantly fighting to stay alive whenever he would leave the Forgotten Castle. One day he went away from Princess Ivy on a quest to find the Magic Flowers."

"The Old Knight was exploring an ancient volcano when he came upon a cave…"

"A dark smelly cave!" cried the boy.

"And being brave and knowing that the Magic Flowers only grew on lava beds, the Old Knight slowly crept inside. He didn't make it very far because he was stopped by…"

"A huge Lava Monster!" "With a lava boulder for a tail!" "That has a loud scary roar!"

"Yes! The Old Knight wasn't scared though because he knew Kung-Fu and carried a huge sword, and the reason his armor was pink was because it was magical and could block any fire from hurting him."

"The Lava Monster roared a terribly loud roar, and the Old Knight used his Kung-Fu moves to silently slip past without ever having to hurt the beast."

Mumbled disappointment came from the boy.

"The Old Knight continued down into the dark smelly cave and with each step he grew more confident because..."

"The cave was lit by glow worms!" cried the oldest.

"His magic armor kept him cool." declared the boy.

"He could smell something sweet!" yelled the smallest.

"That's Right!" Dad said, "The tunnel was lit by billions of shining glow worms along the ceiling and walls, and even though it was getting warmer as he continued into the cave, his armor kept him nice and cool. And he could smell something sweet that was making the dark nasty cave a little more pleasant. The Old Knight stepped into a very large cavern where he saw..."

"Magic flowers!" cried the oldest, followed closely by "A Unicorn!" from the smallest.

Dad laughed. "Yes! There in the middle of the cave were the sweet-smelling Magic Flowers growing in bunches along the edges of the red lava. And standing between the Old Knight and the Magic Flowers was a majestic Unicorn."

"With a rainbow mane!" exclaimed the oldest.

"The Unicorn was all white with a rainbow mane and a glowing multi-colored horn on its head. The Old Knight put his sword point into the ground and bowed his head to the Unicorn showing respect to the magnificent creature."

"And then the Unicorn bowed back!" cried the oldest.

"The Old Knight slowly moved toward the Magic Flowers while the Unicorn stepped aside to allow the Old Knight to pick a handful. They were all sorts of colors, and they glistened as if they had been sprinkled with glitter. The Old Knight then made his way back out of the cave and when he came to the huge Lava Monster at the entrance he…"

"Showed the Magic Flowers to the Monster!" "Threw a flower at the Lava Monster!" "Kissed the Lava Monster on the nose!" came the overlapping cry.

"No, he gave the Lava Monster one of the Magic Flowers to eat and as soon as the Lava Monster ate the flower he turned into a handsome prince named Arthur. He told the Old Knight that he had been turned into a Lava Monster by the Evil Witch and her Gang of Thieves. He was so grateful to be his old self again that he agreed to follow the Old Knight back to the Forgotten Castle."

Dad paused for a moment to adjust his seat as the three children snuggled in closer.

"The Old Knight and Prince Arthur jumped on Leeony's back and rode quickly to the Forgotten Castle where they found the Evil Witch and the Gang of Thieves about to capture Princess Ivy. The Evil Witch was casting a spell to freeze the entire castle and the Gang of Thieves was surrounding the castle ready to fight."

"But what about the pet dragon?!" asked the boy.

"That's good, son. Toasty the dragon was using his fire-lightning breath and rainbow powers to confuse the Evil Witch and her Gang of Thieves. Luckily the Old Knight had the Magic Flowers and when he threw one at the feet of the Evil Witch she immediately started..."

"Dancing!" "Glowing!" "Singing!" came three loud exclamations.

"Yes!" Dad said. "The Evil Witch started to glow, then she began to dance, and once she started dancing she began to sing. Her ugly robes became a bright gold shimmering gown and the evil look on her face became soft and gentle. The Gang of Thieves immediately asked for forgiveness and pledged to serve the Old Knight, the beautiful Princess Ivy and the handsome Prince Arthur for the rest of their lives."

"And do their laundry!" said the oldest.

"And do their dishes too." said Dad. "Very soon afterward the Forgotten Castle was lively and new with bright white and gold decorations. King Gregory of Everlastia returned and on an exquisite spring morning the Princess Ivy and Prince Arthur were married. The Unicorn came to live with them too and they all lived happily ever after."

"The End!" the three children cried.

"Oh, not yet." Dad said. "The Old Knight retired and started a farm on the slopes of the burning volcano. He used the power from the Magic Flowers to grow the best crops in the land. People came from far away just to buy his pumpkins and carrots and rutabaga."

"Daddy, what's a rutabaga?" asked the little one.

"It's a vegetable." Dad answered, and then continued, "The Old Knight had the most delicious apples, and the sweetest corn, and no one could match the crispness of his potatoes or the deep, dark green of his kale."

"Dad, what?" cried the boy, "Kale?!?"

"Yes, kale, which is absolutely delicious when grown together with Magic Flowers."

"Gross!" said the boy, making a face.

"Now that, children, is the end!"

Dad started to move and the children all piled off the big puffy blue chair. He walked them to their beds and kissed each of them on their forehead as he tucked them in. Mom came in to kiss them goodnight too and then stood with her arm around Dad in the doorway.

"Goodnight children. I hope your dreams are filled with Unicorns and Magic Flowers tonight."

"Daddy?" The littlest one asked. "Are you the Old Knight?"

Dad chuckled. "No, sweetheart, but the Old Knight rescued me." he said with a wink.

21042651R00020

Made in the USA
San Bernardino, CA
31 December 2018